DEDICATED TO EVERYONE
WHO BELIEVES IN CHRISTMAS

Story *by*

K. C. MCKINNON

Cover Art *by*

CECELIA COX

Chapter Art *by*

KAY BLACK

Book Design *by*

TARA MCKENZIE

Copyediting *by*

LAUREL ROBINSON

The colophon art was done by Ethel O'Leary Pelletier in 1934 for a high school class.

ISBN 978-0-692-30948-3

Published *by*
ETHEL BOOKS
Visit us at: **www.EthelBooks.com**

PRINTED IN CANADA
First Printing

A LOVE STORY FROM THE NORTH POLE

"I call you Milly," he said, "because I love that name. Just as I love you.*"*

For Kim-
This is a love story from the North Pole, which sits just atop Allagash.

THE SECRET WORLD OF Mr. & Mrs. Santa Claus

K. C. McKinnon

K C McKinnon
Cathie Pelletier

CHAPTER 1:
The North Pole

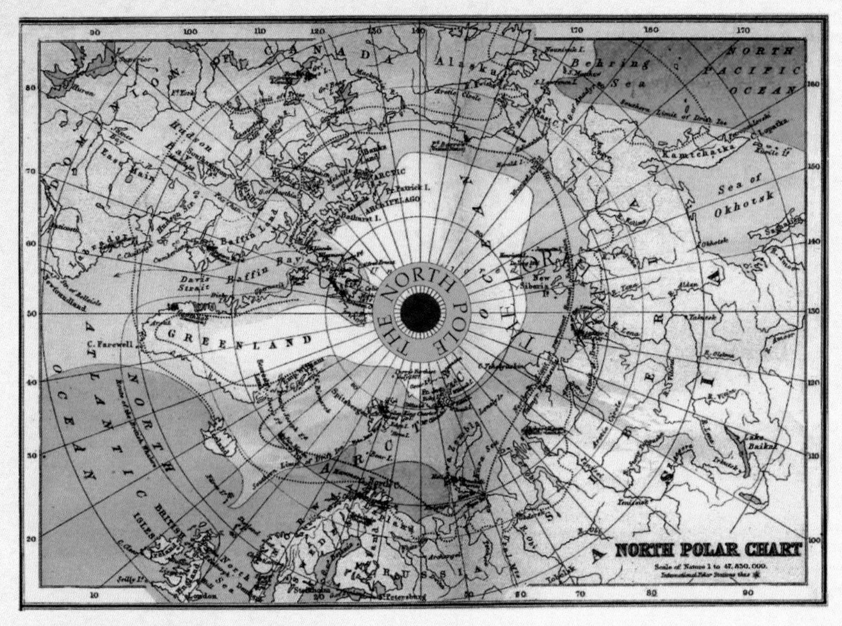

All directions point south when you live at the North Pole.

December 21. He stood outside his house, staring up at Polaris directly overhead. At his feet, a stream of light from the oil lamp on the kitchen table cast a yellow road across the frozen snow, then disappeared into the blackness beyond. Milly would be just getting up, warming her hands at the stove, ready to make breakfast for them both. There had been no sunlight, not even twilight, since the early days of October. He heard in the distant darkness the sound of sea ice shifting, cracking, cakes moving against each other. The South Pole had a land mass to boast of, but he liked something about the danger of where he lived, the sheer stamina it took to survive in the middle of the Arctic Ocean, floating on nothing but dreams.

For too many seasons to count, there had been nothing there but the elves, the reindeer, Milly, and him. And that had been good enough. Then one day human voices were heard in the distance, followed again by years of silence. Then new voices again. Then silence. But he knew they were coming, getting closer with each decade, with each new idea, each fancy invention. He knew civilization for he visited it on that one December night each year. He had seen it as it used to be, quiet and comfortable in its skin. And then the skin started to expand with technology and notions too big for a tiny world. The skin of that old way had exploded, and now, where was anyone safe anymore? Once Chapa, his Head Elf, had come scuttling across the snow, frantic, his red mittens waving like warning flags. "A whale larger than any whale ever in creation!" he cried, his small face showing fear, a rare thing for any elf.

He went to look for himself and saw that it was a submarine, surfaced among the floating ice. "We would be lucky if it were only a whale, Chapa," he had said. Then, "Don't mention this to Mrs. Claus or the other elves."

"Husband?" He had never grown accustomed to the music in her voice. "Your coffee is ready. Don't let my tea get cold waiting for you." It was the kind of voice angels must have. He turned and stared at that place in the sky that would swallow him up in a few days, his first stop at Nunavat, Canada, a mere 508 miles away. All directions point south when you live at the North Pole. Considering that, it was as if his job were defined for him by geography alone. And if you're headed south, perpetually, why not go in a sleigh pulled by reindeer and loaded with toys? He had been born to this destiny, and he accepted it.

From the stables came the snorting of the reindeer, their hooves clamping down on the wooden boards. How they knew, he could never tell. But they did. A week before the journey they became restless, their bodies filling with a need to fly through the night unfettered, with only his reins to guide them. Beyond the stables, a long row of small huts lit up, one after the other, as if they were synchronized fireflies. The elves were getting up. He never knew an elf to be late, yet they had no use for such things as clocks or watches. Even Milly saw the common sense in owning a sturdy clock. "Otherwise, how can we sleep deeply enough to dream?" she had asked, that year he brought the clock back from Zurich as her Christmas gift.

He turned then and stared off at another angle, toward the northern coast of Greenland, his last stop when all the toys had been delivered and he was homeward bound. Greenland was the nearest land to his house and workshop, a place called Kaffeblubeen Island, 430 miles away. The reindeer rested there, and it gave him time to come back to himself, to let the rush of adrenaline that had flown with him around the world subside. He knew Milly would be waiting up for him there at the Pole, and he never liked for her to see him as anything but calm. And then, December 25 was his "Blue Day," as she called it, that one day he and the elves rested. After a year of hard work there was nothing left to do but *imagine* the faces of the girls and boys who got the gifts they had asked for. "Don't be so gloomy," Milly would tell him. "Think of the amazing feat you've just accomplished."

He was more restless than gloomy on the 25th, eager to be back at work for the next holiday season. But having her remind him again of what he'd done the night before always made him smile. To pass the time, he watched the elves celebrate once they had fed the reindeer those special leaves of arctic birches and willows they had saved since summer for the occasion. From his kitchen window, he smiled as they held hands and danced around bonfires they had set to blazing on the ice. Then they sat on their tiny haunches, close to the orange flames that lit up their faces, and ate special little dishes of pudding that even Milly wasn't allowed to taste. They would not see sunlight again until dawn arrived in early March.

By the 26th, everyone was back at work, as if that special night had never happened. The elves would begin mending the harnesses and putting away the sleigh and bells while he checked supplies for the coming year. The letters asking for toys usually didn't begin arriving until late summer. But the elves didn't wait for letters, for they knew the secret hearts of children. The warehouses behind their huts would be half-filled with toys by that time.

"Husband?" She never called him by his first name, and he wasn't even certain he had one. Kriss? He didn't think that name fit him, and he could never imagine his wife calling him Santa. "Chapa is waiting at the back door for the daily list." His Head Elf, his most trusted and respected Chapa, was more his friend than worker. The list would be that day's toys to be made. They had four more days before the magic of that one night. "How can it all fit?" Milly had asked, the first time she watched the elves pack the sleigh. Hundreds of thousands of dolls, a mountain of ice skates and microscopes, enough teddy bears and train sets to fill Yankee Stadium, a river of board games, model planes, battery-operated cars, bicycles and doll carriages, coloring books and regular books, basketballs and soccer balls, baseball mitts and baseball bats, stuffed animals and science kits. Clothing he left to the parents to buy, even if they often signed *his* name on the gift card. He didn't mind. Blame it on Santa if a boy needed a new coat for school.

But yes, how *did* it all go inside that one sleigh? A year's work. That was another reason he knew that his life existed partly because of magic, or maybe wishing. He wasn't sure which. Years ago, he had decided it was best not to ask. If all those millions of children still believed in him, and if that energy alone was enough to conjure him up, who was he to question? It felt real enough to him, the nuzzle of the reindeers' cold noses as he fed them lichen from his hand, the smell of his chimney smoke curling up like a corkscrew, the ice-laced wind against his face over Patagonia. And then, how could Milly not be real? Her hand in his, her warm body next to him as they slept. But his job was not to question, especially in a world where there were no answers.

"Husband?" He heard the door creak wide open this time and saw her shadow fall out across the snow, as if she herself would make that first run to Nunavat. "Are you asking too many questions again about our lives?" She had told him once, hoping it would reassure him, "If they quit believing, if they let the need for us die, then we'll disappear together."

But the bleakest night in his memory had occurred for a different reason. He had been delivering presents, where he couldn't remember, only that it was in some house well-decorated for his visit. Paris? Sydney? Los Angeles? London? A magazine written in English was lying open on a desktop. He had just put the last of the presents under the tree, petted the wide-eyed cat that had watched his every move, and eaten the muffin and drunk the cocoa that had been left for him, when he saw the words: IS THE NORTH POLE IN DANGER OF VANISHING? His hand trembling as he held the magazine, he read the story about sea ice melting, polar bears in danger, and how in thirty years summers in the Arctic could be ice-free. *Thirty years.* It was the worst night of his life, that night in some stranger's house, so far from Milly and Chapa and the elves. But he had said nothing to Milly. What could he tell her? "Even if the children go on believing, there is another danger. Even figments of the imagination need a place to live."

"I'm coming," he said to her now. "Tell Chapa to wait for me in the Main Shop. As soon as I've had my coffee, I'll join him."

With one last look southward, that direction he had been born to, he turned back toward the yellow light of his house, his wife, and the only life he knew.

CHAPTER 2:
The Winter Solstice

"Look, husband, how the purple saxifrage blossoms on the snow."
MILLY'S SCRAPBOOK

December 21. She had awakened just minutes before the clock began its soft chiming. She always woke before he did and lay there listening to the rise and fall of his breathing. Outside their bedroom window was the same black winter sky, endless above endless snow and ice. In autumn, when she knew the birds were gone from the tundra that lay at a latitude below them–whistling swans, golden plovers, snow buntings–she imagined their dark strings in the sky, long necklaces headed south for the winter. She had seen them as eggs and then fledglings, and now they were gone. During the winters, her days were etched in ice.

"Husband, it's time." She felt him stir beside her, his hand reaching out to touch her face. She listened as he rose then in the darkness and found his trousers, the sound of his belt buckle clicking against the cold. He would make the fire that she would later warm her hands to, and then coffee and tea and another day of darkness, until March.

This was the longest and blackest night of all. It was on this night that she yearned most for summer, those softer days before the birds left the tundra and the pale sun had finally returned as promised. She *knew* summer, or the closest thing to it. Every year they made several trips south, journeying far enough that the elves could gather barrels of lichen to bring back to the Pole for the coming year. In single file, and walking on small homemade snowshoes, they filled a warehouse with provisions. Lichen fed the reindeer. "Remember now," Chapa would instruct the others. "Poisonous lichens are yellow." They also harvested hundreds of pounds of moss and the fluffy blooms of cotton grass that they carried back to their huts in small knapsacks to be used in mattresses and as lining in their boots and mittens. It was also fuel, along with reindeer dung, for their tiny stoves.

It was during those trips that they would leave the elves, she and her husband, and he would take her even farther south so she could walk among the crowberry, the bearberry, and the purple saxifrage. True, it was work in that she needed plants and their berries as supplies for the coming year. But he knew she loved those visits for the pure pleasure in them. "Look, husband, how the purple saxifrage blossoms on the snow." Even in June, there was always frost beneath the ground, beneath the arctic rushes and cotton grass, hidden in the earth like a cold heart. She would watch the ruddy turnstones spin in icy pools, their feathers catching drops of water. And the ptarmigans would rise at the sound of her footfalls.

At moments like that, she could forget the night in late December when she worried that he wouldn't come back, that some mishap in the burgeoning skies over Malaysia would take him away from her. Or maybe it would be a wrong turn on the black curve stretching around the Horn. Summer helped her forget. Instead, she thought of the berries she would pick, some for jellies and jams and syrups. Some for their dark dye that she would use on the quilts she was making. Other berries would be dried and ground for her morning tea.

"I've made you a fire, Milly." She heard his voice from the bedroom doorway. "Stay a bit longer until the house is warm." She knew by then that this was her own destiny. She had grown into her life as his wife, the way a path grows comfortable to feet once it has been walked and is familiar. Now, she couldn't imagine a world without him. But it hadn't always been that easy. When she first came to live at the Pole, she despised the elves, all 100 of them, their tiny hammers tapping all year like a flock of crazed woodpeckers. That first year, to keep her sanity, she counted a trillion slaps of their paintbrushes against wooden trains and dollhouses. And then, there was that first Christmas Eve that she was left alone with them. When the elves knew for certain that her husband had disappeared, when the jingle of bells died away in the frozen sky, they nodded to her politely, then slipped back toward their huts, small dark shadows moving slowly across the ice. She was certain they were spying on her, 200 eyes like fireflies outside her bedroom window. But she had been wrong. And with time, she saw them for what they were: tiny hearts born to a world of unselfish servitude.

By the second year, she knew the names of every elf, even their favorite habits. The elderly Chapa liked to nap for five minutes each day at noon, so long as he could lie on the soft lichen in the stables. Benmo, the tiniest of them all, would take his weekly bath in one of the wooden pails the reindeer drank from. Peento, Dram, and Tollah collected stamps from all the letters sent by children from around the world. At the end of the workday, they would spread hundreds of colored squares on the huge table in the Community Hut. "Look!" Dram would cry out, holding up a stamp in his small hand. "This one is from a brand new country!" Freech loved to yodel, Yankta to hum, Geeza to sing, Copkov to knit, Kildin to count his own fingers over and over, and Mealo to skip rope, which was made from braided moss. She knew them all, on and on, the ones who crocheted rugs with guard hairs the reindeer shed over the summer months, the ones who played homemade wooden harmonicas, and the ones who studied the same stars night after night, from September to March, stars that, like the sun, bounced on the horizon but never set.

She dressed in darkness, in her faded jeans, a blue flannel shirt, and the heavy sweater Copkov had knitted for her during the summer months. The skeins of dark blue wool that made it had come from Australia. In the kitchen she made the coffee for her husband, ground from Brazilian beans, his favorite. And then her own special tea, brewed from cloudberries she had picked down in the tundra or, sometimes, from the leathery leaves of the bearberry, with its silky hairs to protect it from wind and cold. Chapa had taught her to always leave the roots of the plants for the next harvest. When the mugs were full and steaming, she went again to the door.

"Husband?" she said, searching the darkness until she saw him. He was studying the sky. Days before his journey, the sky pulled him to it, as if whispering to him in a voice only he could hear. "Your coffee is ready. Don't let my tea get cold waiting for you."

She went back to the kitchen and took baked bread from the oven of the woodstove. It was made from the flour he had brought back from some city, the name of which she had already forgotten. She brushed the hot loaf with olive oil and then spooned out a bowl of her crowberry jam. They always gathered those berries on their last trip to the tundra each autumn, after the first freeze, when they tasted sweetest. Chapa had taught her how to arrange the fresh crowberries on a cookie sheet, cover them, and then put them in the hut used only for freezing foods. All her tundra berries and nuts and plant leaves were shelved neatly in the Freezer Hut. When the sun came back in March with its twenty-four-hour days, she rejoiced by making *akutuq* from cloudberries, an ice cream dessert the Inuit invented. In celebration, 100 wooden bowls with long handles would be lined up in the Dining Hut, and each elf would eat the dessert with a handmade wooden spoon.

Right on time came the soft rapping at the back door. When she opened it, Chapa smiled up at her, his aged face showing its wrinkles proudly. At three feet high, he was one of the taller elves. But the years had worked over his bones, and it seemed to her that he was smaller each time he came for the daily list.

"Reindeer impatient this morning," he said, in that murmur of a voice all the elves had, as if a breeze were moving through wind chimes.

"Tell them it's only four more days," she said. "Surely reindeer can count."

Chapa nodded, a crescent of smile filling up his small face.

"Maybe I will teach them," he said, and reached up to take the chocolate she offered him each morning. "The list, Missus?" he asked. She watched as he squatted on his heels, the bar of chocolate held firmly in both hands as he nibbled at it.

"I'll tell him you're here, Chapa."

She closed the door and left him to enjoy the sweetness of his treat. Just as the sleigh carried acres of toys when it left, it also carried supplies for the long year ahead when it came back: needles and thread, a rug for her feet from Persia, chocolate from Belgium, a small piece of turquoise from Arizona, magazines and a book of poetry from England, a bracelet made of shells from Jamaica, maple syrup candy from Canada, and even a fancy bottle of perfume, once, from Paris, that made her blush at the sight of it. She would never ask to go with him one Christmas Eve, just to see for herself. She knew it was not his fault that she was left behind. It was the way they had invented him in stories and poems and legends. She herself came later, as if she were Eve coming to soothe the lonely Adam.

"Husband? Chapa is waiting at the back door for the daily list."

But if she couldn't go and see for herself, she could at least dream. At night, she never dreamed of polar bears or owls white as snow. Instead, she dreamed of parrots brilliantly blue and orange and red. She dreamed of pink flamingos and long-necked giraffes, and gray elephants lifting their ivory tusks against the savannah night. Once, she dreamed of a saguaro cactus, its green arms raised in surrender beneath a red desert sky. At first, she craved color the way vampires crave the red of blood. But now, she could see the color white for what it was: a soft blanket to curl up in and sleep. So she taught herself early on how to dream. And dreams had saved her.

"Husband, are you asking too many questions again about our lives?" He thought too deeply, especially at that time of year when the sky beckoned to him and the reindeer pawed the floors of the stable.

"I'm coming. Tell Chapa to wait for me in the Main Shop. As soon as I've had my coffee, I'll join him."

When she closed the door this time, she leaned back against it and breathed deeply. She needed to quiet her heart before she spoke again to Chapa, who would just be finishing his chocolate. She needed to tell her heart over and over, "He will come back safely again this year. He will come back this year. He will come back."

CHAPTER 3:
The Beginning

If an elf sees more than one iceberg, he must remove his bonnet and sing the Chant of Icebergs backward.
THE ORAL HISTORY AND TRADITIONS OF ELVES

Each time he stepped inside the Main Shop the excitement made his ears buzz, as if a million bees were at work instead of 100 elves. On those occasional times when he walked alone, far from the buildings and Milly and the elves so that he could think by himself, he was always stunned by the sheer silence of the North Pole. As far as he could see, no matter how he pivoted on his heel, it was a world of ice, ice molded and chiseled into glassy blue shapes, mounds, and ridges. But no sound. No human voices or calls of birds. The contrast now of the noise in the Main Shop, where all of the toy construction took place, was the exact opposite of the silence nature had intended for the Pole. He opened the door to the rattle of saws buzzing, nails being hammered, drills drilling holes, and toys being tested for their quality, a clatter and clamor that he knew was a well-organized chaos.

Chapa came scuttling out from a sea of lumber, paint cans, brushes, and cans of screws and nails. Spread out on a large table behind him were some of the many designs from around the world that Dram, Peento, and Tollah used to design the traditional toys that were always made each year. Their interest in stamp collecting had grown from their knowledge of countries and customs.

"You're moving fast today, Chapa, for an elf your age," he said, smiling at the small shape before him. Chapa nodded, and then pointed at the table of designs that were being sorted by a dozen elves assigned to traditional toys.

"Dram is most concerned about time, sir," Chapa said, his breath coming in short puffs. He had always reminded him of a tiny train perpetually making its way uphill.

"When has Dram *not* been concerned with time?" he asked. Every year, on the winter solstice, it was the same fear as the countdown grew closer.

"But they haven't finished with the *kokeshi* or the *matrioshka*," Chapa insisted, his mouth twisting comically as he pronounced the words. "The dolls for Japan and Russia. And then we are 5,000 short on the worry dolls for Guatemala."

"As we are every year at this time," he said, smiling again at Chapa's caring face. How many years had he known him as his friend? Too many, and that was another kind of countdown that pained him when he thought of the future. "And as it has been for all these many years, the elves will again work miracles."

"And the stuffed koala bears," Chapa insisted, checking down the list he had been given that morning. "We are 8,000 short. And the jump ropes, sir? We are behind 6,423. Benmo and those with the smallest fingers are working on them now. But there are many still to braid."

"Much to do and yet four days still to go," he said, and put a calming hand on the old elf's shoulder. He felt the frail bones beneath his fingers, beneath the moss-woven coat that all elves wore. He had grown thin with age, Chapa had, brittle with worry. Of the many incorrect things written about those who live at the North Pole and bring Christmas to the world, one of the most humbling was that elves never age. They *did* age. He knew it. Milly knew it. And most important, Chapa knew it. "All is well, old friend. Each year this concern runs like fire among you. Perhaps I should have 100 worry dolls from Guatemala made so that I can give one to each of my elves for Christmas."

When Chapa laughed, it was a sound like no other he had heard in his travels around the world. It was more a series of snorts and wheezes, followed by a long, satisfied sigh.

"All is well, sir," Chapa said, bowing as he did to show his respect to the man who towered above him. Then he returned to the table that was smothered now in more designs: the wooden-and-leather drums and spinning tops bound for Mexico, carved red Dala horses for Sweden, guitars and sling shots, bags of colored marbles and wooden whistles and building blocks.

He never asked how Chapa and the elves did it. He only cared that they did. He stood watching them, how well they worked together, each seeming to know when it was his turn to design a wagon, or varnish a baseball bat, or string a toy necklace. It was as if they communicated in some silent language the way he had read insects do, nodding in agreement to each other although words had not been spoken, one elf handing a paintbrush to another, who reached for it simultaneously. Or a small hand passing a hammer to an elf who grabbed it without even looking up from his work.

As he stepped from the Main Shop, he saw her blue coat just disappearing into the Christmas Library, as she called it. He smiled at this, but it also saddened him. He had hoped long ago that she would learn to trust the night that lay ahead for him. She would trust his well-trained reindeer to pull the sleigh, trust the sturdy harnesses that the Stable Elves had worked on long and hard so that they were strong enough for the journey, trust the reins in his hand to give the reindeer perfect direction. Most of all, he wished she could learn to trust *him*, his experience, and his need to come home to her safely.

In the stables he put his hand beneath the nose of the reindeer in the first stall and let it smell his warm skin. Its facial hairs, meant to protect its muzzle when grazing in the snow, tickled his fingers. He could feel the excitement exhaled in the breath coming from its nostrils. Four more days, and then imagine the run, their legs working feverishly in long strokes against the sky, as if they were swimming through air. He hadn't named them as the many poems and stories claimed, especially the most famous poem by Clement C. Moore. And he didn't own eight, nor did he own nine, with Rudolph coming later, in 1939, when Robert May wrote the story of a reindeer with that name. He and Milly had laughed together the first time he brought her back the poem "A Visit from St. Nicholas." It was in an old copy of the *New York Sentinel*, dated December 23, 1823, and the poet was still anonymous then.

The year he brought that newspaper home must have been 1850. He couldn't remember exactly, only that she had been with him for a year then. From the beginning, it was her nature to seek knowledge. That was the year she had started the library and begged him to bring her anything and everything that mentioned either of them. "Oh my, it says you have a belly that shakes when you laugh like a bowlful of jelly," Milly had said, on that December 25 morning so long ago. "Maybe you should quit eating my bread." He never minded her teasing. "And here's where you talk to the reindeer. 'Now Dasher, now Dancer, now Prancer and Vixen!'" Milly read the words aloud.

"It really says that?" he had asked, leaning over her shoulder to read for himself. "That's what they think I say? Why would I do that? The reindeer have no names." But she was happy with the newspaper, and that was all that mattered to him. "'On Comet, on Cupid!'" She looked up at him. "Cupid? The god of love?" she asked.

He took the newspaper from her hand to read for himself. "But two are named Donner and Blitzen," he said. "That's *thunder* and *lightning* in German. I rather like the sound of that."

He had twenty sturdy reindeer, and the Stable Elves took the best care of them. He respected his animals. He saw that they were well fed, watered and groomed, well stabled, and exercised daily. They were a single unit that thought as one, so he did *not* name them, which would only individualize and weaken them. But if he had, there would be no Prancer or Dancer! The job they did in pulling a sleigh loaded with a universe of toys, the precision in getting it around the world, landing over and over again on rooftops and other structures, and then back to the Pole on one night, was serious business. At least for him and the reindeer it was. But for the poets and dreamers, for little children and adults with young hearts, their Santa was *that* Santa. So he didn't mind the poem, even though it referred to him as a *jolly old elf,* which made Chapa snort and wheeze and sigh in one huge laugh. He rather liked the poem. Let them enjoy the myth, the legend, the folklore. After all, they had created it, and he was thankful for that.

And then, in the artwork Milly had been saving, he was often drawn standing tall in the sleigh and cutting a bold arc against the sky over some chimney. Standing up in a sleigh moving that fast! He almost wished Clement C. Moore could try that trick himself, just once. And while he *did* have hair that came down to his shoulders, it was not white, but brown mixed with gray. And couldn't the artists start drawing him trimmer and slimmer, as he truly was? Working year-round, except for that one day of rest, working in the cold of the Arctic, who could stay that fat? Whales, maybe. And then, he had always hated beards. He would rather glue reindeer moss to his face. But it was worse for Chapa and the elves, who had giggled and wheezed for hours the first time they saw a painting of themselves. There they were, with pointed ears and bells on the tips of pointed caps and shoes. What self-respecting elf would dress like that?

Were all their lives that fragile, that they were built on nothing but fanciful words?

CHAPTER 4:
Milly's Library

To her amazement and joy, there were dozens of beautiful flowers and shrubs, such as the arctic poppy that always turns its face to the sun.
MILLY'S SCRAPBOOK

In the Christmas Library she read the spines again, all those books he had brought back over the many years, just as she had requested. "Why do you need to know, Milly?" he had finally quit asking her. And she had quit asking him, "Why do you call me Milly? My name is not Milly, or even Millicent. Nowhere, in any of these pages, have I been given a name." She had swept a hand that day to indicate the rows of shelves that lined the walls before her, shelves that had grown full over the many years: hardcover books, softcover books, magazines, newspapers, films, even photographs and artwork. "I am just

Mrs. Claus, a plump old woman in a red dress. And look at the spectacles on my nose! Husband, please tell me you don't see me that way!"

Of course, he didn't. She had changed with the ages, with the styles, even if the myths kept her locked to an image. And he had changed with her, adapting to jeans and leather boots, shirts and modern coats. It didn't matter to him so long as he was warm and could do his tasks easily enough. "All right, so we started life in our fifties and we're probably going to be in our fifties forever," she said, although she had never spoken of the loss of her childhood, her teenage years, her young womanhood, or turning thirty, then forty, then fifty. Just as he never spoke of his own loss. "But I don't have to look like Mary Todd Lincoln, or Carrie A. Nation, or even Mamie Eisenhower. I can look like women my age look *now*."

It was true. And she did, in her jeans and boots and colorful sweaters. She had asked for things, and he had brought them back to her so that she could feel a part of each new age. When her old-fashioned scrapbook had been filled to bursting, he brought her a very modern red one. And there were the pieces of simple jewelry, tiny earrings and a garnet ring, the lipsticks and eye shadow, the occasional purse even though she had no use for one. Other things that she would never ask for he brought anyway, such as the case of honey-brown hair dye that he left in the library for her to find. Now her hair could be the way she wanted it for another year. "Why do you call me Milly?"

He had taken her in his arms that day and held her tightly against his beating heart. "I call you Milly," he said, "because I love that name. Just as I love *you*."

Her personal library had grown over the decades with the elves constructing more and more shelves for her, twice expanding the building itself. Now she felt there was little more she could add, unless something new was published. None of it was true, of course. It was more a combination of *all* folklore, beginning in Scandinavia, then moving slowly to America and the famous poem "A Visit from St. Nicholas." There were origins for elves and their cousins, the gnomes. And origins for the tradition of a bearded man going from house to house with gifts. Sometimes he was riding in a cart pulled by a goat. Other times he walked. Sometimes he left sacks of coal for bad children. There were so many variables from country to country that no one was right, and yet everyone was right. Like the moon and stars, the residents of the North Pole belonged to the entire world, to *all* people.

She loved the library. It was the quiet place where she worked on her scrapbook of tundra flowers and plants, making notes about them. Chapa had taught her many things, such as how the permafrost is just a finger's length below the Earth's surface, even in summer, so tundra plants cannot put down long roots. And yet, to her amazement and joy, there were dozens of beautiful flowers and shrubs, such as the arctic poppy that always turns its face to the sun. Some plants had dark red leaves to help them absorb the sun's rays each brief summer. She kept details on the elves in that book, too, how their bonnets were made of woven arctic rushes, their coats of knitted moss. And how they insulated their mattresses and mittens with the white tuffs of cotton grass. Because cushion plants grew in the shape of small cushions, those were used as pillows under their heads. She had collected liverworts, hornworts, purple saxifrage, crowberries, cloudberries, heaths, and many of the various lichens, that favorite food of caribou and musk oxen. She pasted their leaves and flowers onto the pages so she could study them throughout the year.

The library itself she had divided by subject matter: CHRISTMAS, SANTA CLAUS, MRS. CLAUS, ELVES, and REINDEER. It was her own passion, her own hobby, just as Kildin loved to count his fingers and Yankta to hum. During the year, she read each of the books that he brought back with him. And each year new titles filled newly constructed shelves. There were Christmas stories about grinches, angels, good children and bad children. There were alphabet books about Christmas, counting books, recipe books, mystery books, and even rubber books that floated in a baby's bathwater. There were books about Christmas dogs, cats, cows, horses, pigs, and turtles. Some stories, such as one about a little girl who sold matches, made her cry. After all, the child dies on Christmas Eve, the most important night at the North Pole. And then, there was never a more powerful letter than the one titled, "Yes, Virginia, There Is a Santa Claus." She had torn the page it was on from some magazine, and now kept it in a plastic sleeve so that the years would not discolor the paper. She knew each word of it by heart. Other books made her happy that there was such a thing as Christmas in the first place, stories of hope, like *A Christmas Carol* by Mr. Charles Dickens. Every time she read the lines "God bless us every one," her eyes welled up with tears.

But what she was seeking most, and dreading most, was a book in which he didn't come home one Christmas Eve. A story that awful and that tragic would have to be written by a heartless author. Writing it didn't mean it would come true, of course. So much of what was written about them was silly fiction. But what if one book was so powerful that it punched some kind of hole into the legend and everyone on earth started believing it? Would that make it powerful enough to change things? But no such book had been published so far. And each year, knowing that he was watching her from a distance and worried that *she* was worried, she slipped the newest books and films onto the shelves and rested easy until the next Christmas Eve.

CHAPTER 5:
It Has Been Written

If an elf sees arctic terns circling overhead,
he must dig a hole in the ice and bury a piece of reindeer lichen.
THE ORAL HISTORY AND TRADITIONS OF ELVES

He walked down the row of huts, twenty-five of them in all. They were actually igloos made of wood. Four elves slept in each hut, each one with two sets of bunk beds, a tiny rocking chair, and a woodstove. Moss and reindeer dung that fed the stoves were stored in wooden bins outside each hut. The bunk beds were built on stilts three feet off the floor to take advantage of the rising heat, making short ladders necessary for the elves to crawl into their beds at night. Mattresses were filled with the fluffy heads of cotton grass that had been gathered in the summer tundra and were made new each autumn. All food consumption took place in the Dining Hut, so there was no need for tables and chairs. But elves love to rock, so each hut held one tiny chair. Since tradition has it that elves can rock only one at a time, for safety and protection, there was no need for more than one rocker per hut. He often teased Chapa about this. "What do you fear will happen if two of you rock at once? A whale will surface from under the sea and snap your chairs in two?" But elves never break with tradition.

How and *when* and *why* had all their traditions started? Nothing like this was written in any of the works Milly had stored in the library. So where was the book that said an elf must drop to his knees if a leaf blows across his path? There *were* no leaves at the North Pole. Even on their treks south to the tundra, there were no leaves. The trees there were gnarled shrubs. "Because that is how it has been written," Chapa would insist each time he was questioned.

"Written *where,* Chapa?" At this question, the aging elf always pointed at the library.

"In *The Oral History and Traditions of Elves,*" he would protest.

"But that's only because you appointed two Scribe Elves years ago and told them to write *The Oral History and Traditions of Elves*. They wrote what you told them to, Chapa. Doesn't anyone remember how those beliefs started?"

This would set Chapa to rocking back and forth on the balls of his feet, from one foot to the other, showing his agitation. "They must write it down before I die," he would insist. "They must write it down."

As much as he admired and respected his Head Elf, this answer only riled up his own agitation. "It's true that elves age, Chapa. We've seen it with our own eyes over the years. You were young when we first met. But maybe elves don't have to *die*. Have you thought about that? Maybe it's just because you all *believe* they do. Just scratch that line out of the book you commissioned the elves to write."

But nothing he said mattered to the little body that stood before him, wagging a finger of caution. "We must never question what is written, sir. We must never question."

In *The Oral History and Traditions of Elves* it was written that the elves live to be 200 years old, and then they die. An elf funeral is held at the edge of the icy sea, as tradition holds. Then, as if by that magic they all lived by, a novice elf will appear to fill the required quota of 100 elves at all times. "But where will the new elf come from, Chapa?" He wasn't being quarrelsome. He *wanted* to know. He wondered the same things about himself and Milly. He wasn't sure how old he was, or even how old Chapa might be. He suspected the elves were older than he since the books Milly had filed in that section of the library gave them a much longer history. But no elf had died before, so he wasn't sure if they were mortal or immortal. The famous Christmas poem by Clement C. Moore was already 190 years old itself. So he had always used 1823, the year of its publication, as his own birth year.

Still, the elves respected and religiously adhered to their *it-has-been-written* list of rules. At noon each day, when all work ground to a halt and they stopped to eat their daily meal, he and Milly were never invited to the Dining Hut. But he had watched from his window as they filled their bowls from the cauldron that burned in front of the long row of huts. In the morning, the ones who were that day's Kitchen Elves had already filled the huge pot with their secret ingredients. He recognized some of the contents that went into the porridge: the fluffy white puffs of cotton grass they had picked on one of the pilgrimages south to the tundra; reindeer moss, so named for its resemblance to tiny antlers; arctic poppies, with their flowered yellow heads; and lastly, liverworts and hornworts, those simple plants that lack leaves, stems, or roots and so can adjust to tundra life. He had been told that the recipe was committed to memory by the Head Elf so that it was safe from theft. He doubted anyone would steal it, not even the reindeer. The huge cauldron was then filled with melted ice water from blue chunks carried back from the open sea.

"Let's hope they never *do* invite us to dine," he had said to Milly, who watched with him one day as the elves got ready to eat.

"Oh, I wouldn't mind tasting it," she said, smiling. "Just so I'd know."

When the Pole had continual sunlight, from March to October, it was amusing enough to watch the elves preparing to eat. But during the sunless months, when the flames beneath the caldron flicked up high and orange against the night, and the stars shone down bright and cold from overhead, it was like watching a dream unfold. At noon, the cauldron would have bubbled and boiled and simmered enough to be ready. The elves then formed four rows of twenty-five elves to a row, Chapa always at the head of the first row. One row at a time they filed past the large black pot and dipped wooden bowls with long handles into the steaming mixture that had become a green mush. Then they each selected one of the 100 small cakes, shaped like mushroom caps, from a table next to the pot. One behind the other, they disappeared into the Dining Hut, where fifty sat on each side of the long table. Songs would be heard coming from within, chants really, that Chapa had explained were hymns of thanks for their food, and for their safe and happy lives. It was Chapa's job as Head Elf to use this time to pass on his vast knowledge, which included the harvesting of tundra plants, how to freeze berries, and the best way to preserve reindeer dung as fuel. And, oh yes, to drop to one's knees should a leaf so much as blow across an elf's path.

When they left the Dining Hut a half hour later, 100 clean bowls with long handles would be hanging from 100 wooden pegs against the back wall. At the door, they turned in different directions, some to the stables, some to the Main Shop, some to the various warehouses, some to the Sleigh Hut, some to the Harness Hut, and some to empty and clean the steaming cauldron, then cover it with a sheet of moss until it was fired up again the next morning. Elves ate once a day at noon, except for December 25, the day that Milly filled their wooden bowls with *akutuq,* the special ice cream dessert made from her cloudberries. Sometimes, he envied them their lives, so ordered and precise and simple. Or, as Chapa liked to say, "Our lives are the way it has been written."

CHAPTER 6:
December 22

"I am just Mrs. Claus, a plump old woman in a red dress. And look at the spectacles on my nose! Husband, please tell me you don't see me that way!"

With the light from the Swiss clock falling across her cheekbone as she slept, he reached out and put his fingers there, caressing her. He lay staring at her face, which had never changed in all the years he had known her. She was that age when she first appeared to him, as if his sheer loneliness had conjured her up. How had it happened? Did he wake to find her lying beside him? Had he stepped into the kitchen one morning, wishing he knew how to make a perfect cup of coffee, and found her standing there, the steaming mug in her hand? Had she simply appeared out of the darkness of sea and sky? He couldn't remember now. But he knew that the two of them, and the reindeer, were made from a different magic than the one that had made elves. They and the animals had never aged a day in all those years.

He heard her sigh, still deep into her dreams, and wondered where she was just then, what she might be doing. Sometimes, he felt almost jealous, knowing she went to those internal places without him. Was she happy as his wife? Was she content in that world of ice that was more twilight and darkness than yellow sun? She was the only woman there, and she often mentioned this herself. Among all the beating hearts at the North Pole, counting elves and reindeer and her husband, she was the only female. It seemed unfair, especially as the years unwound and women grew more and more important in the eyes of the world. That's why he had begun taking her down to the tundra in the summers so she could see pairs of birds creating homes and families for themselves. It was all he had to offer, meager as it was. But she loved those summer journeys. She would lie on the ground next to her favorite flowers and stare up at the puffy clouds that dotted the sky like cotton grass. Did she yearn for children? She had never said so. Once, he had asked her that question. She had merely smiled and said, "But the elves are my children, husband, all one hundred of them."

He put his arm over her, feeling her warmth. It was always a gift to wake and find her next to him. But he needed the touch of his lips against her face, his fingers moving through her hair, her body blending into his as they slept. How would he have managed, year after year, without her? He wouldn't have. He knew that now. When the clock began its soft chiming, he did what he did every morning of their life together. He closed his eyes and pretended to be asleep.

"Husband, it's time."

He kissed her face, then left her cuddled in the warm bed.

"Stay until the house is warm," he said. "I'll make the fire."

It was after Milly had risen to warm her hands at the stove, and make his mug of Brazilian coffee and her mug of cloudberry tea, that the expected knock came at the back door, right on time. He opened it to see Chapa standing there, his small moss coat tied shut with braids of reindeer hair instead of buttons, his bonnet pulled down over his ears.

"The list, sir?"

"Why do you need to come each day for the list, Chapa?" He had asked him this question many times over the years, just to tease him. "I can bring it to the Main Shop when I've had my breakfast."

"Because it is written," Chapa said, rising on his heels to reach for the bar of sweet chocolate that Milly was offering him.

"And is it written that my Head Elf must have chocolate each morning?" he asked, only to have Milly slap his hand lightly, urging him to stop. But Chapa had already gone down on his haunches to nibble at the treat. When he finished, he wiped his tiny hands on his coat and stood, his thin fingers reaching up.

"The list, sir?"

This was the day they brought the sleigh out for cleaning and preparation. A group of ten elves worked in unison, throwing open the doors to the Sleigh Hut and pulling the large vehicle forward on its massive runners. At twenty feet long, it was much bigger than depicted in holiday art over the decades. And it sat atop four gigantic runners, two to a side. The inside had been lined with thick blankets woven of reindeer hairs since each deer shed 5,000 outer guard hairs every summer. He inspected the frame as the elves waited with their cans of red paint. Each year they painted it so it would be fresh and new-looking. And that was as fine a color as any, if the world's children wanted Santa's sleigh to be apple red. But it was a two-seater, and most of the likenesses he had seen were of a sleigh with one seat, in which he stood and sometimes flourished a whip. He would *never* whip his reindeer. He had the reins there to guide them. Once they left Nunavut, that first stop, they were already flying like a single engine, their hooves pounding against the air currents that rushed beneath their bellies.

The first task concerning the sleigh was for him to inspect it. Not that he didn't trust the elves and their learned knowledge, but he was the pilot. And any good pilot makes sure his ship is ready. He examined the runners first, checking for wind abrasion. Because the runners were straight, he could travel only forward and in a straight line. Piloting a sleigh wasn't easy, even on ground snow. Turns have to be thought out well ahead and taken as wide and slow as possible. He checked the shafts next, to make sure they hadn't cracked, even though the old ones from last year had already been replaced by the Sleigh Elves. He liked the shafts to be hefty since they could handle more stress when he turned the sleigh. He would check them again just before he left, when the reindeer were in their places and the harnesses fitted. That was the usual time shafts might split or crack, by being stepped on by many elves during harnessing.

He liked the looseness of the sleigh's body. Unlike carts and wagons, sleighs were built to shift and flex. He checked the undercarriage next. Since it was made mostly of mortise and tenon joints, it presented a weakness for damage. Ice and rain coming at him, some of which was now acid rain, were enemies of the undercarriage. But there was also the sand over the massive deserts of the world, grit and dirt, factory soot and smog and smoke. The sleigh's dashes looked fine. All that was left was the metalwork and bells, to give it that Christmas appearance and sound. Four elves were in charge of bells, which were always shaft bells, his preference, twenty bells fastened to a strip of wood that was carefully screwed into the shafts. He never doubted the elves would fix any problems with the sleigh should any occur. But part of his job was to be certain. It was up to him to take these fine and trusting animals up into the night sky, whisk them around the world, and then bring them back safely.

Six of the elves came forward then, carrying the heavy canvas bag. It was fitted snugly into the backseat of the sleigh. When opened, it was into this canvas mouth that all those toys disappeared. How did that happen? Milly had searched every inch of the bag, every crevice and corner, looking for even a tiny hole or a small tear. “Where does it all go, husband? How is it possible?” He didn’t know. He had no answer. But the following day the elves would finish making the last of the toys. Then the reindeer would be exercised and put through their paces. And the morning after that, Christmas Eve Day, the ritual of loading the sleigh would begin. Millions of toys and presents would go into that one canvas bag.

And the rest was, well, *history.*

Milly's Akutuq Ice Cream

(AH-GOO-DUCK)

The recipe has been used by indigenous peoples for thousands of years. It was first considered a "traveling food" essential for survival, especially when men were out hunting. Traditionally, the grandmother or mother of the successful hunter made the akutuq *(also called Eskimo ice cream) for ceremonial feasts and funerals. Modern versions use vegetable shortening instead of tallow, and have added raisins and sugar. At the North Pole, this ice cream dessert is served only on Christmas Day.*

Ingredients:

1 cup solid vegetable shortening
1 cup granulated sugar
2 cups freshly fallen loose snow
(or ½ cup water or berry juice)
4 cups fresh cloudberries

Directions:

In a large bowl, cream vegetable shortening and sugar until fluffy. Add the two cups of snow (or water or berry juice) and beat until well combined. Fold in berries, 1 cup at a time, until blended. Place in freezer to firm up before serving.

Preparation time:

15 minutes

CHAPTER 7:
December 23

If an elf sees a falling star, he must sing his name aloud so the star will know it is not alone.

THE ORAL HISTORY AND TRADITIONS OF ELVES

He made a fire in the woodstove and then stepped out into the darkness to study the sky. As they did every morning, the firefly lights in the huts flickered on, one after the other, as the elves climbed down from their bunks and turned on the oil lamps. Chapa's hut lit first, a tiny yellow light in the one small window. Then the next hut, and the next, and the next. Perfect harmony. Perfect synchronization. It would be a busy day for them, and he worried whether Chapa would be up to the task. Each morning the old elf seemed a bit slower in overseeing that day's work. His heart hadn't faltered, but his body was tired.

And it was getting more difficult with each passing day for him to hide that fact from the others.

He and Milly had discussed it often as the holiday season grew near. They had even tried to shoulder some of the responsibility of supervising the daily jobs by offering their help. But Chapa would have none of it. "Only the Head Elf can give advice or instructions to other elves!" he would scold them. "It has been written."

He was sorting over letters on the table, a few last stragglers arriving just in time, when the knock came at the door.

"I'll be darned," he said, looking at the clock. "He's almost a minute late." That had never happened before.

"Don't tease him this morning, husband," Milly said as she put his mug of coffee on the table. But elves knew nothing of sarcasm, so Chapa was not affected by the teasing, or even aware of it. Still, if Milly was uncomfortable, he would do as she wished. When she opened the door, Chapa's wrinkled face grinned up at her.

"The list, Missus?"

"Husband, Chapa is here for the list," she said. Then she went to the cupboard and took down the tin canister where she kept the bars of her best chocolate. Both hands reached up quickly, the thin fingers clutching each end of the bar. Then down he went on his haunches to nibble. Elves never said *please* or *thank you*. Those words did not exist in their vocabulary. Being so eager in their hearts to serve others, and to share all that they owned, there was no need for such terms in their world. Even a word like *friend* was never used, since all elves were perpetually kind and generous to each other.

"These are the last of the letters, Chapa," he said after the old elf had finished his treat and wiped his hands on the moss-woven coat. "Nothing here to worry about. If I counted correctly, we already have overstock for the presents that are asked for."

Chapa reached for the letters and quickly shoved them into the pocket inside his coat so that they could rest against his heart. Elves called this their Heart Pocket. His small round eyes closed slowly as he *imagined* the new toys and presents that were being asked for in those envelopes. No matter how many times she had seen it, it always made Milly smile when it happened, when an elf *visualized* the wishes and prayers of children. *If an elf closes his eyes, he will see in his mind what is written on any paper that is pressed to his heart.*

Chapa opened his eyes and released the big sigh that meant relief.

"Yes, it is good," he said. He pushed his hands back inside his mittens with the cotton grass linings. "We have all the toys they asked for already made in the last warehouse."

"I'll join you shortly, Chapa, old friend," he said. He used the word *friend* often, for it was the best one he could think of when it came to his Head Elf. "No more worries now, for those were the last envelopes. The post office to the North Pole is officially closed for the holidays."

"I will be waiting, sir," said Chapa. He hobbled out the back door, and it closed behind him. Elves never put front doors in their huts. Nor did they use them in other buildings. *If a knock comes at the front door, it will bring with it a year of sadness. A front door is the only door bad fortune can enter through.*

At noon, the Reindeer Elves had put halters on the animals, and now they led them out of the stables, one behind the other. The sounds of snorting and the grinding of hooves against frozen ice filled the darkness. Their hooves, divided in half and forming an almost perfect circle, gave them great traction on snow and ice. And they needed traction for the take-off on Christmas Eve. From the inflatable pouches of skin under their throats, once used to amplify their bellows when searching for a mate, loud barks and grunts could be heard. The reindeer were impatient, ready to be put through their paces.

Fifty sticks wrapped with oil-soaked moss and lichen had been driven into the frozen earth behind the stables. The sticks zigzagged in two rows across the snow. Four elves ran forward, each carrying a torch that had been lit from the flames beneath the cauldron. Down the rows they went, two to a side, lighting the moss-and-lichen sticks until all fifty of them burned brightly, flambeaus against the darkness. The wavering light cast by the flames marked a slalom course. Now the Reindeer Elves led the twenty deer behind the stables and began putting them through their paces. They needed to be reminded of how the sleigh must turn slowly, the arcs anticipated. But the memory of seasons past came back quickly, and in no time they were swiftly executing perfect turns, some of them gliding as though they longed to take to the air that very moment.

He had been watching the magnificent sight from the upper end of the stables, standing back in the shadows to see how the elves handled his team. The huge antler sets of each deer shone smooth in the orange flames of the torches as they repeated the course again and again. They would shed those antlers in January, and the elves would rejoice at the many tools and utensils to be made from the cast-offs. Their massive legs moved gracefully, as if they were swimming in water. But they were good in water, superior swimmers because of the way their thick undercoats–13,000 wooly hairs per square inch–trapped air between the coat and skin, making them buoyant. This physical trait guaranteed even more buoyancy when airborne, when swimming across the open sky. With those strong legs, a day-old calf could outrun any healthy man. A superb creature, the reindeer.

He watched as one of the Reindeer Elves approached Chapa, bowed, then made motions with his hands toward the herd, his red mittens now almost orange in the flickering firelight.

"Reindeer are ready, sir," said Chapa, coming to stand next to him.

"Chapa, they look remarkable," he said, and put his hand on the elf's shoulder. Again, he felt the frame of bones holding up a structure that refused to go down. At least not yet. "Old friend, I wish you could come with me tomorrow night on my run."

He heard the wheezing and snorting at just the thought of this, an elf accompanying Santa as he delivered toys! But at least he could still make his Head Elf feel cheerful.

That night in bed she lay in his arms, their last night together before he left to fly around the world.

"Will you be warm enough?" She asked this every year.

"Of course. The reindeer blankets that Copkov knitted are so heavy, I have a good mind to throw them overboard, especially when I'm above the Gobi or the Sahara."

He loved making her laugh.

"Don't even mention such a thought to Copkov! He's been knitting since February."

"I'll be warm enough, love. Don't worry."

"Shall I pack you a basket of food this year, just to be safc? What if something unexpected happens?" She asked this every year, too.

"If you knew how many calories are left out for me, Milly, all around the world, you wouldn't be worried about me getting hungry. Fat, maybe, but not hungry."

It was true. They left him a reservoir of hot cocoa. A mile or two of toast and croissants. Enough oranges and grapefruit and apples and mangos and pomegranates to fill a thousand orchards and groves. He often brought fruit home to her, such a delicacy at the Pole. In Denmark, where he was known as

Tomte, the children left him *risengrod,* a rice pudding. In Kenya it was a plate of roasted goat. In the Philippines, he would find *queso de bola,* a ball of Edam cheese that he could wash down with more cocoa. In Chile, he was left a sponge cake stuffed with candied fruit called *pan de pasqua*. In Britain and Australia, he was given sherry to wash down mince pies. In Ireland, he also got mince pies but a pint of Guinness there. In the Netherlands and France, food was left for the reindeer instead of Santa, fat carrots, sweet hay, and even bowls of water.

He thought she had fallen asleep, and so his mind drifted to the next day's work and what lay ahead. It was never really nervousness he felt the night before a trip. But there was anticipation that sometimes bordered on anxiety. He knew how the reindeer felt in their stable stalls. He could hear them right then, even though the stables were beyond the warehouses, the dull clop of hooves against wooden floorboards, the occasional snort and grunt. It was still just ten o'clock. He knew the elves would rise at midnight to begin packing the sleigh. They worked around the clock on that one night, as it had been written.

He felt her stir in his arms and so held her more tightly.

"Husband?"

"I'm here."

"I could never live without you."

"I know. That's why it will never happen."

CHAPTER 8:
December 24

It was time for him to leave. Five minutes to midnight.

The sleigh was ready, freshly painted and sitting in front of the first warehouse. The large canvas bag in its backseat was now open and waiting to be fed. At midnight on the 23rd, the elves rose, put on their woven coats and knitted bonnets, then turned down their oil lamps. All but Chapa would be in assembly line mode for packing the sleigh. To get everything loaded, they would work around the clock, midnight to midnight, until his departure. Two dozen large lichen-and-moss-bound torches were already driven into the packed snow to light the way from the warehouses to the sleigh.

He had awakened at midnight, and with Milly still sleeping, he stood at the window and watched as the first toys were carried out of the warehouses. A bicycle came first, passed down the line of small hands until it disappeared into the canvas bag. Immediately behind it was another bicycle and another and another, over and over until all the bicycles were loaded. He went back to bed. He knew that thousands of dolls would come next, in what seemed to be an unending string. After the dolls would be the baseball mitts and then the microscopes, the castanets, miles of stuffed teddy bears wearing red bows, and on and on.

Over the summer and autumn months, as each letter arrived, the elves assigned to gift cards had already printed the names of each child for each present. Below the name was "Merry Christmas" in the appropriate language. Years ago, Milly had hung a chart in the library with the proper Christmas message for each country. Often he would see the elves studying the chart throughout the year as they wrapped the presents and wrote the cards. *Chuc Mung Giang Sinh* for Vietnam, *Glædelig Jul* for Denmark, *Selamat Hari Natal* for Indonesia, *Sung Tan Chuk Ha* for Korea, *Nadolig Llawen* for Wales, *Sawadee Pee Mai* for Thailand, *Craciun Fericit* in Romania, *Joyeux Noel* in France, *Feliz Natal* in Brazil, and *Geseënde Kersfees*, which was Merry Christmas in Afrikaans. It always amazed him that every country of the world had children living there who believed in Christmas, and who believed in *him*. It was not true that the nice ones got the gifts while the naughty went without. It hurt his heart to think anyone could believe he would judge a child, for he knew that children are mere vessels filled with ideas from the adult world around them.

The next morning, when he had built a strong fire in the stove and Milly had made their morning coffee and tea, he stood at the window, watching through the frost on the panes. The elves were still busy at work, now packing the musical instruments, toy pianos and guitars, clarinets and drums.

"How are they doing?" Milly asked. She had come with her steaming tea to stand next to him.

"It looks like they're right on schedule," he said. They would stop at noon to ladle the green mush from the cauldron, give thanks for the food by chanting, and then file out of the Dining Hut and back to work. Ninety-nine elves, with Chapa looking on and giving instructions, working twenty-three and a half hours, unceasing, no sleeping, no rocking in the one rocking chair in each hut, only working to pack the sleigh. And still, he had no idea how it was possible that they managed to do it. It was as if an ant decided to move a mountain of dirt in a single day.

At five o'clock he showered, and he then sat at the kitchen table while Milly brought the special supper she had prepared. She'd been planning it for days and had been cooking much of the afternoon, shooing him from the kitchen if he stepped inside for a cup of hot tea to shake the chill. Now she brought a dish of appetizers, small pastry shells filled with onion and some kind of herbs he guessed she had picked in the tundra. Delicious. And the steaming pot of soup, filled with potatoes and carrots and peas she had put in the Freezer Hut from his journey last year. They never ate animals, and wouldn't have even if animals had been available at the Pole. The whales and polar bears and seals they saw on occasion were like amazing visitors to them. They couldn't imagine killing such rare friends. And then, the eating of animals would distress the elves greatly. *An elf cannot eat a living thing that has a heart, for an elf can hear the thoughts of every heart.*

She brought the potato pasta next, his favorite of all dishes. He watched as she spooned a creamy tomato sauce over his serving. The loaf of hot bread was put in a basket and left near his hand where he could help himself often. She knew he loved her bread.

"Eat, husband," she said, pulling back her own chair and sitting across from him. She poured them each a glass of wine from the bottle she had saved for that night. The flame of the candle she had lit earlier danced gently to the breath of her words. He raised his glass.

"To my wife," he said, "and to this night."

For dessert, they ate fat pieces of crowberry pie and drank freshly made cups of coffee. She reached a hand out and touched his face.

"Have you eaten enough?" she asked.

"I feel like taking a nap now," he said, teasing her. But instead, he did what he did every Christmas Eve. He went to the gramophone he had brought back to her in the early 1930s, put her favorite record on, and then cranked the thing up. With no electricity at the North Pole, a gramophone was the perfect answer. He offered her his hand, and she accepted. As they waltzed, their bodies close, Ruth Etting sang "Why Dream on a Night Like This?"

"What special gift can I bring home to you this year?" he asked.

"A kitten," she said, so quickly that he realized she had been waiting for him to ask. A kitten? He thought of the probability of bringing a live animal in the sleigh. The magic worked for him and for the reindeer, but would it work for a creature from the world of humans?

"Milly," he said, touching her hair. "I don't see how that's possible."

"I know," she said, as if anticipating his reply. "Of course, it's not practical. A new coat then? I'm tired of the old one."

A soft rap came at the door. Milly went to open it and found Chapa standing there. He only came to their house each morning for the list, no matter how many times they had invited him for an evening of food and conversation. It was not the way of elves to leave the company of other elves for their entertainment.

"Missus," he said, "I need to speak."

He left the table and came to beckon the old elf into the room. "Chapa, my friend," he said, "step next to the stove and warm yourself."

Chapa shook his head. He moved closer so that Milly wouldn't hear.

"It will be Dram," he whispered, his hand patting the special pocket inside his coat, the one that was sewn so that it would rest above his heart. "I have written it."

And then, before Milly could offer a bar of chocolate, not knowing if he would accept it at that time of day, he turned on his small heels and scuttled into the blackness outside. Through the opened door came the excited voices of elves still loading the sleigh. It was seven o'clock. They had five more hours of work. Milly closed the door.

"What in the world was that all about?" she asked. "Chapa has never done that before."

He didn't answer, but he knew what it was about. Chapa had told him earlier in the week. "As it is written, I will choose an elf to replace me when my times comes."

But he had pushed it aside as pointless talk. "Chapa, you will live for many more years. If you are tired or weary, certainly an elf can replace you. They call that *retirement* out in the world of people. That means you can spend your days working on a hobby. I know you would be very good at checkers, and I would be happy to teach you how to play."

But Chapa had looked into his eyes and said again, "As it is written, I will choose an elf to replace me when my times comes."

At half past eleven, the Sleigh Elves came as always to knock at the back door and announce that things were on schedule. Twenty-five more minutes and the last of the toys would be loaded. The Reindeer Elves were bringing the team out of their stables now.

He had finished dressing in his red parka with the fur-lined hood. Despite the famous Christmas poem, red was a good color for that kind of terrain. He wore heavy mittens on top of berber-lined gloves, and two thick pairs of socks inside his snow boots. Milly had also dressed in warm clothing. They followed the Sleigh Elves out into the night, the air around them cracking with cold.

"Where is Chapa?" he asked, for the old elf was not standing at the sleigh, overseeing the packing. Benmo, the smallest of the elves, stepped forward.

"Sir," he said, "Chapa is in his hut and has asked if you have a moment before you leave tonight."

Of course he had a moment. He had whatever his friend needed and asked for. With the reindeer panting and pawing the frozen snow behind him, he walked to Chapa's hut. Milly came with him, but at the door she hesitated.

"You should have some time alone with him first," she said.

Once inside the tiny hut, he had to bend for fear of hitting his head. Chapa was lying on a bottom bunk, his eyes open and staring upward. Dram was rocking in the one rocking chair and chanting a litany so soft, it was almost unheard. It sounded like a prayer, one he had not heard before from the elves. When Dram saw him bending in the arched doorway, he quickly stood up from the rocker. It stopped rocking instantly, as if it had been given a command.

"I will be at the sleigh now, sir," Dram said. Grabbing his bonnet from a wooden peg, he scurried out the door. Chapa raised his head, his eyes acknowledging the visitor. He knelt by the bedside. He couldn't stand straight in that small hut, but it was better this way. He wanted to be able to look into his friend's eyes at this important time.

"You will not be seeing the sleigh off tonight?" he asked. Chapa shook his head, but did not reply. He reached a hand out from under the blue blanket that Copkov had been knitting for the past month. The blue dye had come from crowberries that Chapa had taught Milly how to pick.

"My friend," he said, and took Chapa's offered hand. It was so small, he was reminded of a child's hand. So small, and yet it had done so much work for others in 200 years of unselfish labor. How many children had been made happy each year thanks to that hard work? He looked again at Chapa's face, the furrows of the years bedded into the skin, the round dark eyes that seemed weary, ready to shut for a final time on the dolls from Russia and Japan, on the braided jump ropes, the drums from Mexico. How many toys had those aging eyes approved, making certain each was perfect?

"Must this be how it is written?" he asked softly, and saw Chapa nod. The hand squeezed his now, a grip tighter than he would have thought possible in that moment.

"Keep tranquility in your heart," Chapa whispered.

The door to the hut opened, and Milly came in quietly and knelt by the bed.

"It's Missus," she said softly, and placed her hand on the blue blanket. *It has been written that a funeral blanket must be the color of water and sky*. "I'm here, Chapa."

Chapa nodded to recognize her presence. His mouth curved into the crescent smile he presented to her each morning before reaching up to accept the chocolate. Outside, the clanging of bells rang loud and clear. The Sleigh Elves were announcing that the packing was finished and the team was harnessed. It was time for him to leave. Five minutes to midnight.

"I'll stay, Chapa," he said then. "I can make up time over the Pacific Ocean. There are air thermals there you can't imagine." But the old elf seemed agitated at the sound of these words. He raised his head and the eyes stared into his. He had learned long ago how to read Chapa's eyes.

"You must go, sir."

"Then I'll see you when I return. I'll bring you a present. I've read that Belgium makes 170,000 tons of chocolate each year. Do you think that will be enough for you, Chapa?"

Chapa lay his head back on the pillow that had been stuffed with cotton grass.

"The wind is strong tonight," Chapa said now, his voice a whisper. Milly glanced over at her husband. There *was* no wind. He had just commented to the Sleigh Elves that lift-off would be easy since there would be no resistance. But Milly knew what to say just then.

"Yes, it certainly *is* strong tonight, Chapa," she said. "The wind will carry you, won't it?" She had seen reference to this in the elf book of traditions in her library. *When an elf has finished his work and his time has come, a strong wind will carry his spirit home.*

Chapa closed his eyes. "I am almost there," he said.

Milly rose first, tears falling silently down her face. He followed. But before they stepped out of the hut, they heard a soft word spoken from the bunk, a word they would take with them for the rest of their lives.

"Friends," whispered Chapa.

CHAPTER 9:
The Good-bye

He and Milly had laughed together the first time he brought her back the poem "A Visit from St. Nicholas."

The reindeer heaved together, and he felt the sleigh move under him, the friction of runners against ice slowing it at first. Then it pulled free, the ice letting it go, and he knew that it was ready. Milly ran forward, as she always did, and reached for him with both arms. The elves lowered their heads, giving them privacy. He held her against his chest, then kissed the strands of hair that had fallen in her face. She would have the awful job of tending to this recent development, and yet, no one loved Chapa more than she did. But he knew that she could handle it. That's why she was his companion, his love, his wife forever.

"Do you know why I call you husband?" she asked, her voice so low only he could hear. "Because I love that word, just as I love you." He took her hand in his and kissed the tips of her fingers, her hands freezing now.

"Put on your gloves, wife," he said, and saw her smile at the sound of the word.

"You're about to fly around the world in freezing temperatures and in zones that will make the sweat trickle down your neck, but you worry about *me*?"

"Put on your gloves," he said again. "I'll be home soon."

She stood back and waited. He nodded to the Reindeer Elves, who quickly let go of the bridles and stepped back. The Sleigh Elves also stepped back from the sleigh. Now the reindeer reared up as if prancing, all twenty of them, the puffs of frozen breath coming from their nostrils in great snorts. A ripple of excitement washed over the elves, a tinkling sound as they gasped. No matter how many times they had seen it, it still astonished them. They circled around Milly and waited. Now the other elves came too, and joined the circle. They watched as he shook the reins almost tenderly. But with that command the huge sleigh moved forward, the ice and snow giving it up to the darkness above. Faster and faster as eighty hooves cut into the ice for traction, and then the liftoff as the runners treaded air and the reindeer swam in unison.

Below him, the orbs of fire from the torches grew smaller and dimmer, until they disappeared. Ahead, he saw those twenty magnificent backs working hard beneath the harnesses, heard the grunts in unison as they pulled. Jets of wind thrust out from beneath their bodies. In no time, he would be landing in Nunavat.

Standing next to the burning torches, they could still hear bells jingling against the sky, growing fainter. And then, in the wake of the sleigh, just frozen silence. He was gone. Milly felt a small tug at the hem of her coat. She looked down to see Dram's sweet face looking up at her. He was second oldest to Chapa and the most learned, curious about all things. Dram knew not to pick the yellow lichens. "They are poisonous," Chapa had warned, every year without fail. And he had learned how to sort and freeze the crowberries, how to gather the best moss for reindeer feed, and cotton grass for the mattresses and mittens. He knew how to make the special pudding the elves would eat on the following day, their one day of rest.

"Missus?" Dram said in his small, musical voice. What had she always thought when she heard their voices? That a breeze was moving through chimes. She knew without asking what he was waiting to tell her. "The wind has taken Chapa home."

She followed him back to the wooden igloo that was Chapa's hut. Inside, a new elf she had never seen before was rocking in the one tiny chair, back and forth, back and forth as he chanted a prayer. Where had he come from? Had he been born of sea and sky? The blue blanket, the very one she had shown Copkov how to dye with juice from her crowberries, covered the rigid body on the bottom bunk. The new elf stood, and when he did, the chair beneath him stopped rocking. She had asked Chapa, once, how that could happen so fast. And he had answered, "Because no one is sitting in the chair, Missus, it has no need to rock."

"I'll be waiting at the library," Milly said to Dram, who nodded.

She sat before the globe that was on her desk in the library. She looked at the clock and figured he had landed long ago at Nunavat. That was the first stop and the closest place for inhabitants. He was probably already airborne again and somewhere over the Pacific Ocean. She never asked for details of the route, and he never offered them. She wondered if he even knew it himself, or if the magic that lived in their lives took control of the reins. Asia would surely receive him first. There were believers in all time zones of the world now, so he would need to start where Christmas Eve arrived first. Stopping at Nunavat was simply ritual to him by now. She thought of the names and places and imagined him flying above them: Papua New Guinea, Australia, Indonesia, the Philippines, Vietnam, Thailand, India, Saudi Arabia, all of Africa, South America and Central America, then Europe, and back to Mexico and North America. Then the northernmost landmass of Greenland before coming home to her again. At least, staring at the globe in her library, she *imagined* his trip would go something like that. Maybe she was wrong. Maybe it all happened in an instant.

As she waited for word from the elves, she felt the sadness of the night envelop her. It was not just the loss of her husband. This Christmas Eve there was a new sorrow. She went into the Elf Section and took down the big book that Chapa had instructed the Scribe Elves to write, a history of their traditions and ways. It was not forbidden to her, but since it had been written so carefully in tiny elf scrawl, she had rarely opened it in all those many years.

"'If an elf sees his reflection in the ice,'" she read aloud, "he must spin three times on his heels.'"

So *that* was what they were doing when she would see one of the elves who was fetching water suddenly drop the pail and start spinning. "Where do your names come from?" she had asked Chapa once. He answered, "It is the chant each of us makes inside while we work." So she had then asked, "Why can't I hear those sounds too, Chapa?" He had merely hunched his small shoulders and said, "Maybe because they are made inside our hearts, and our hearts are very tiny." *If an elf sees his shadow during daylight days, he must lie facedown on the snow and count to ten. If an elf sees a falling star, he must sing his name aloud so the star will know it is not alone.*

She flipped through the pages, stopping now and then to read the proper way to line mattresses with cotton grass, how to groom the reindeer and gather hairs at the same time, how to clean the tiny long-handled bowls, how to make the cauldron fire using moss and dung. On the last page, a line caught her eye since it was freshly written in a different ink, loosely scribbled, and not in the neat hand of a Scribe Elf. *The Head Elf requires a square of chocolate each morning when he goes to fetch the Daily List.*

As she read the words, tears in her eyes, a knock sounded on the library door. Dram had come to tell her it was time.

Stars had broken through the black sky overhead, and now they glittered with cold. The elves had made a litter of braided moss, as it was written, with woven handles on each side for carrying. Ten of them acted as pallbearers, five to a side. As it was also written, Chapa's small body lay on the moss frame beneath the funeral blanket Copkov had knitted. Dram was standing in front of the procession, holding a large torch and waiting. Behind were the rest of the elves, forming a long line and each carrying a smaller torch. She was not allowed to follow them to the edge of the open sea, and she had accepted that rule when Dram explained it to her. Only elves could be in attendance. This was their first funeral. Who was next? Dram himself, most likely.

As the procession began, slowly, carrying the precious cargo, she was surprised to hear her own voice call out to them.

"Wait, please!" she cried.

All 100 elves stopped in their boots and watched as she ran from the steps of the library, out across the frozen yard, and into her house. Hands shaking, she pulled down the tin canister from the cupboard shelf and took off the lid. She grabbed a bar of the chocolate he had loved so and raced back outside. No one spoke as she walked over to the litter and put her hand in under the blue blanket. She left the bar of chocolate to rest against his silent heart, hoping that he would know it was there, in that way Chapa had of knowing so many things.

She waited in the library while they were gone, *The Oral History and Traditions of Elves* opened in front of her, its pages turned to "Elf Funeral Rites." She was not allowed to attend the ceremony, but she could at least *imagine* that she was there by reading the words. The elves assigned the task of carrying the body would bear it to the edge of the sea. The new Head Elf would then reach into the Heart Pocket beneath Chapa's coat and take out the piece of paper with a name written on it, in this case *Dram.* The paper would be lit by the Head Elf's torch and thrown burning into the sea. This would make the change official. They would then speak the words they knew in their hearts, all 100 elves chanting in unison under the stars, remembering Chapa's good and long life: "One with sea and sky, one with sun and stars, one with every child, and one with us who knew you." And that's when the wind would carry the precious body home. When Dram lifted the blue blanket, there would be nothing beneath it. He would then toss the blanket over the ice-rimmed edge and into the sea.

She was sitting on the steps to her house, waiting, when the elves returned with the empty litter. Their 100 glowing torches danced in the night like fireflies. Dram was walking in the lead, where Chapa had once walked. Without a word to her or to one another, they began driving those glowing torches into the frozen earth, creating a runway. Then the assigned elves put them out, one by one. A few hours later, when they expected the sleigh to return, the torches would be relit.

She stood and shook the chill from her body. There were still things to be done. She went inside her kitchen and began making the special ice cream.

CHAPTER 10:
The Return

"Do you realize what you have done tonight?" he said aloud to the team.

He could never tell anyone, not even Milly, how he did it. He didn't know himself how it happened, and in such a short time. He remembered the night in bits and pieces, as he had remembered that magazine article and the wide-eyed cat that watched him, in a house on some street on the planet Earth. Bits and pieces. But surely he didn't land on every rooftop in every country. How many small houses, and in some countries mere huts, could hold the massive weight of his sleigh and his team? Was it one rooftop for each country then? He didn't know.

Often, he could recall only names when he tried to reconstruct the journey: a boy named Tomica in Croatia; Ingrid in East Germany; a boy named Alexei and his sister Valentina, in Russia; a girl named Paadini in India; a boy and girl named Johnny and Aihe, in Australia and New Zealand. He remembered smiling at the thought of Benmo's small fingers doing such intricate braiding when he left identical jump ropes for twins named Rossa and Palantina, in Papua New Guinea. But that was it. When it was over, it was as if he woke from a trance and Kaffeblubeen Island, in Greenland, was looming beneath the pounding hooves of his reindeer. So how *did* it happen?

On Kaffeblubeen Island, he lit the torch that had been stored below the canvas bag by the Sleigh Elves. The hard-packed moss burst into bright flames against the night. He watched as the reindeer walked in frantic struts, their legs getting accustomed again to earth beneath their hooves instead of sky. He himself would do his own pacing, letting the adrenaline fade away as best he could. He then checked the hooves of each deer and saw that they were fine, no frozen ice clogging the hairs there. Walking among his herd, he put an assuring hand beneath each of the twenty muzzles, feeling the hot breath against his skin, letting them know that he was proud of them, patting their fine necks and stroking their backs.

"Do you realize what you have done tonight?" he said aloud to the team. He was answered with snorts and grunts and barks, the perfect language of reindeer. But they *knew,* just as he knew. He took a sack from the sleigh of that most desired treat of reindeer, the leaves of arctic willows and birches. The Reindeer Elves would never forget such an important item. One by one, he fed his deer from the sack, listening to the sounds of chewing and now gentle stomping. By the time the sack was empty, they were calmed, ready for home and a long night's rest in the stables.

He was ready for home, too. He turned and looked toward the north, at Polaris, for when you live at the North Pole, everyone on earth must look in that direction to find you. Was he invisible, as it seemed? The day the submarine had surfaced, frightening poor Chapa, no one seemed to notice him standing there at the water's edge, his Head Elf at his side. And the men who came to shiver as they shoved their country's flags into the frozen ice looked right through him, as though he were a ghost. And the planes that flew overhead never seemed to spot him, or his numerous warehouses and huts. Instead, they cast shadows from their wings down onto the frozen snow, shadows that even passed over him as he stared upward. Yet no one had seen him. Not yet, anyway.

And that's when the article came back to haunt him: IS THE NORTH POLE IN DANGER OF VANISHING? Thirty years. Just thirty summers for Milly to trek south at his side to pick her berries and marvel at the tundra's flowers and birds. Surely it wasn't true. Surely his life would go on as always. There would be his day off, what Milly called his "Blue Day," as they ate the sweet ice cream made from cloudberries. One day off, and then another year of work ahead. It had never bored him. Every doll, year after year, seemed different. Every train set seemed headed for different towns from the year before, every microscope revealed a new secret world. How had he come to be so lucky that he could do this job year after year, with a woman he loved at his side, both of them never aging? He could only hope his luck would hold.

Before he took up the reins again, he reached far down into the canvas bag, now loaded with things Milly could use in the year that stretched ahead. He felt the warm ball of fur, still curled and sound asleep. Next to it was a second ball of sleeping fur. He had seen the two starving kittens on some street, lingering at a garbage can, their thin sides and sad meows making his mind up in an instant. South America? Mexico? The United States? Portugal? He couldn't remember now, only that it had been on one of the last legs of his journey. He had fed them warm milk from a glass left waiting for him at his next stop. The milk, he remembered, sat next to a doughnut and a note that began "Dear Santa Claus." His fear that they might not survive in the sleigh was now gone. One woke and licked his hand with a warm tongue, then curled next to the other and fell back asleep. So magic works for kittens, too. How could it not? He covered the flap of the bag to keep the cold air from entering. What good was one kitten alone at the North Pole? He imagined her face. He would tease her at first, telling her to please reach into the bag for the oranges he had brought her.

By the time they were airborne again and Greenland was already behind the sleigh, he had put the magazine article from the year before out of his mind. He should never have read it in the first place. He would tend to the things he had control over, those things he could change. He wished he had been at Chapa's side to the end. But Christmas Eve waits for no man, and no elf. Everyone knew that. He thought of the North Pole without his dear friend and knew that he was not free of sadness as people imagined him. *A jolly old elf*. Chapa had been his friend and helper for 200 years.

And more sadness would come. Dram and Benmo and Copkov and Kildin. It was obvious that the other elves were fated to the same kind of transience. All he could do was what he knew best. He would read the letters, make sure the toys and presents were ready, and then deliver them to the waiting children whose hearts would fill with happiness. He would continue to enjoy the little things in his life: his morning coffee and the sound of wind moving through chimes when one of his elves spoke.

And he could rejoice at his love for a woman named Milly, who had been at his side for so long now that he could not remember life without her. A woman whose eyes filled with wonder at the sight of ruddy turnstones spinning in icy pools, the pale sun catching water droplets on their feathers. And ptarmigans rising on sturdy wings at the sound of her footfalls. A woman whose delicate fingers gathered cloudberries and who was at that moment making the yearly bowls of sweet ice cream. Milly, his wife, whose eyes filled with love and pride each time she looked at her husband. He gave thanks for those blessings, for unlike the elves, his world had a need for *please* and *thank you*.

One thousand feet up, but knowing she would be able to hear the distant bells, he gently tugged at the reins. His team answered immediately, and the mighty sleigh turned in a magnificent arc, the North Star bright over their heads. In seconds he saw the runway looming out of the night, the tiny dots of orange flames burning brightly on the snow below, showing him the way through all that darkness, guiding him with love, bringing him safely home.

THE END